Fun Dog, Sun Dog

story by
Deborah Heiligman

illustrations by
Tim Bowers

Marshall Cavendish
New York London Singapore

Marshall Cavendish, 99 White Plains Road, Tarrytown, NY, 10591
www.marshallcavendish.us

Library of Congress Cataloging-in-Publication Data
Heiligman, Deborah.
Fun dog, sun dog / Deborah Heiligman ; illustrated by Tim Bowers.– 1st ed.
p. cm.
Summary: Although Tinka the dog can be described in many ways, she is always the right kind of canine for her owner.
ISBN 0-7614-5162-5
[1. Dogs–Fiction. 2. Pets–Fiction. 3. Stories in rhyme.] I. Bowers, Tim, ill. II. Title.

PZ8.3.H4132Fu 2005
[E]–dc22
2004023789

The text of this book is set in Coop Flaired.
The illustrations are rendered in acrylic paint on gessoed three-ply bristol board.
Printed in China
First edition
1 2 4 6 5 3

For Tinka, and for her friends Honeybee, Marigold, and Trippy –D.H.

To my friend, Jeff –T.B.

Tinka is a sweet dog,
a treat dog,
a jumping-up-to-greet dog.

A fun dog,
a sun dog,
a run-and-run-and-run dog.

A ride dog,
a slide dog,
a stay-right-by-my-side dog.

A beach dog,
a reach dog,
a something-new-to-teach dog.

Tinka is a dandy dog,
a sandy dog,
a snatching-all-my-candy dog.

A howl dog,
a yowl dog,
a crawl-beneath-my-towel dog.

An ocean dog,
a motion dog,
a grabbing-suntan-lotion dog.

A sticky dog,
an icky dog,
an icky-sticky-licky dog.

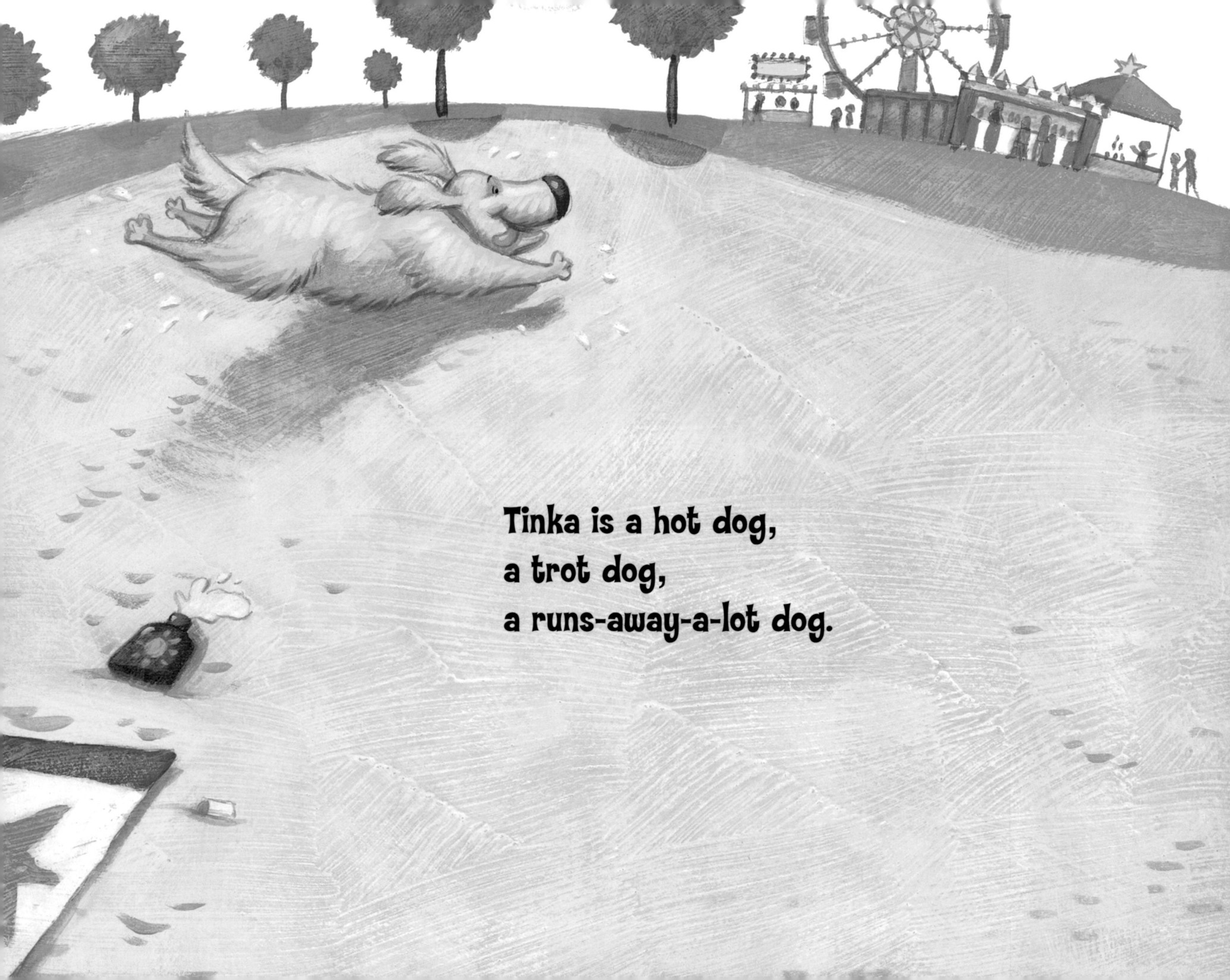

Tinka is a hot dog,
a trot dog,
a runs-away-a-lot dog.

A fair dog,
a bear dog,
an I-don't-want-to-share dog.

A busy dog,
a dizzy dog,
a soda-is-too-fizzy dog.

Tinka is a park dog,
a bark dog,
a take-me-home-it's-dark dog.

A night dog,
a fright dog,
a something's-not-quite-right dog.

A *Hey!* dog,
a sprayed dog,
a skunk-got-in-the-way dog.

Tinka is a stink dog,
a blink dog,
a too-big-for-the-sink dog.

A tub dog,
a rub dog,
a scrub-a-dub-a-dub dog.

Tinka is a prancy dog,
a dancy dog,
a brushed-and-combed-and-fancy dog.

A nap dog,
a wrap dog,
a climb-up-in-my-lap dog.

A care dog,
a share dog,
a when-I-need-her-there dog.